Bear in a Square

L'ours dans un carré

Stella Blackstone
Debbie Harter

Barefoot Books
Celebrating Art and Story

1 Find the bear
in the square.

Trouve l'ours
dans le carré.

one
Un

2 Find the hearts in the queen's hair.

Trouve les cœurs dans les cheveux de la reine.

two
deux

3 Find the circles in the pool.

**Trouve les ronds
dans la piscine.**

three
trois

4 **Find the rectangles in the school.**

Trouve les rectangles dans l'école.

5 Find the moons in the cave.

Trouve les lunes dans la grotte.

five
cinq

6 Find the triangles on the waves.

Trouve les triangles sur les vagues.

six
six

7 Find the diamonds on the crown.

Trouve les losanges sur la couronne.

seven
sept

8 Find the zigzags around the clown.

Trouve les zigzags autour du clown.

eight
huit

9 Find the ovals in the park.

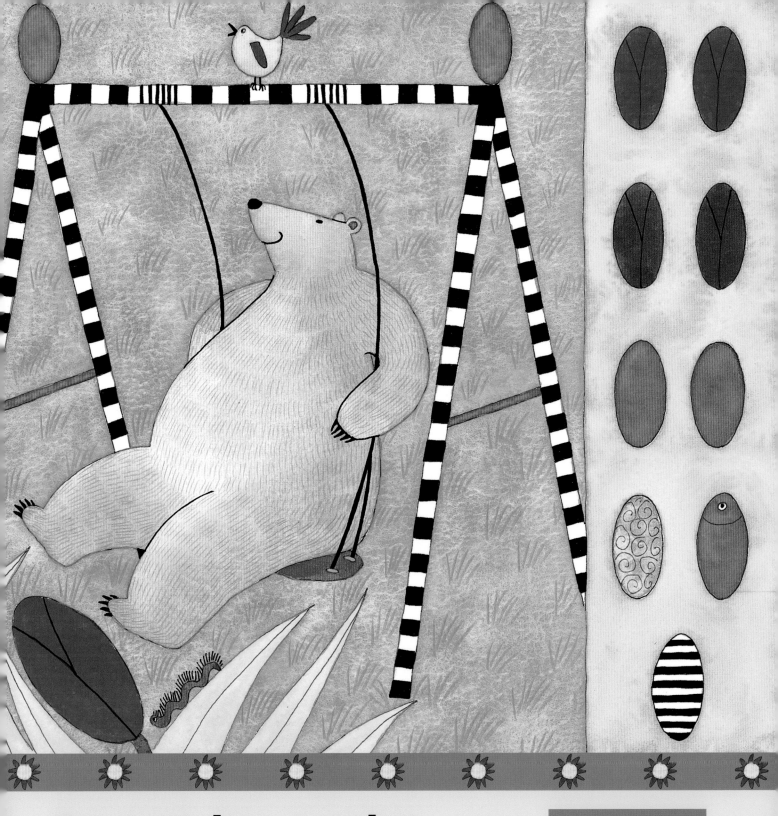

Trouve les ovales dans le parc.

nine
neuf

10 **Find the stars in the dark.**

Trouve les étoiles dans le noir.

ten
dix

blue square

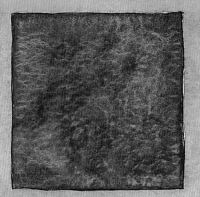

carré bleu

red heart

cœur rouge

green circle

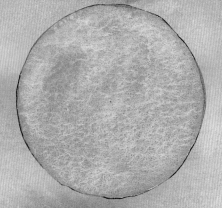

rond vert

brown rectangle

rectangle brun

white moon

lune blanche

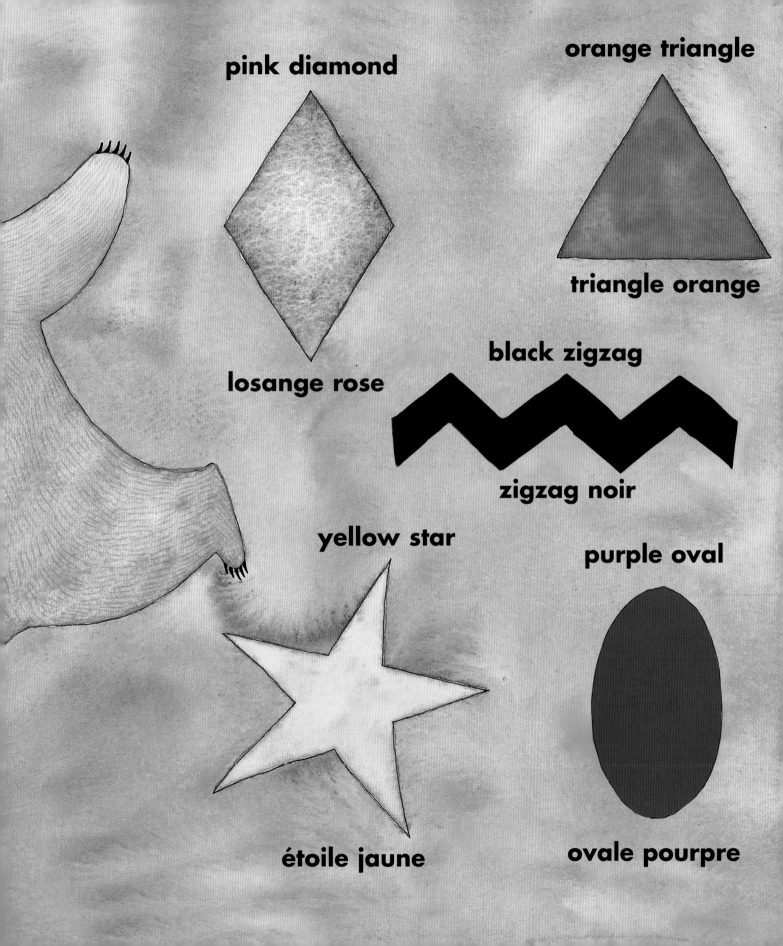

pink diamond

losange rose

orange triangle

triangle orange

black zigzag

zigzag noir

yellow star

purple oval

étoile jaune

ovale pourpre

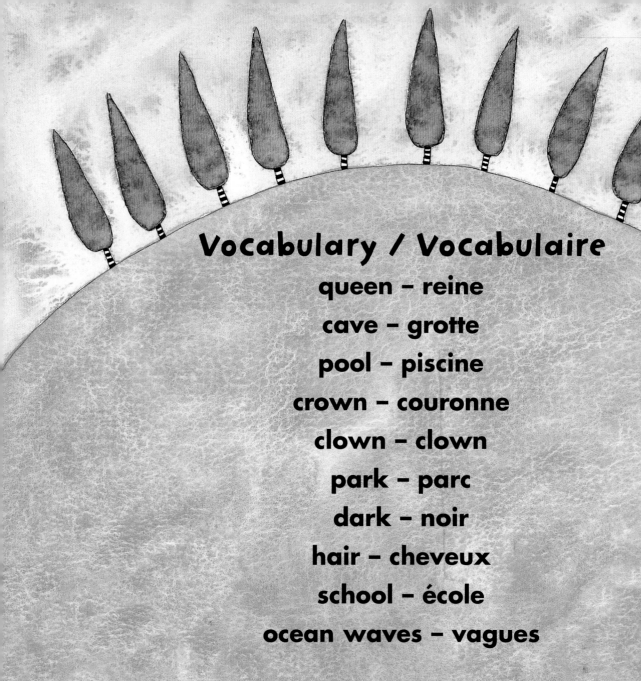

Vocabulary / Vocabulaire

queen – reine

cave – grotte

pool – piscine

crown – couronne

clown – clown

park – parc

dark – noir

hair – cheveux

school – école

ocean waves – vagues

Barefoot Books
124 Walcot Street
Bath BA1 5BG

Barefoot Books
2067 Massachusetts Ave
Cambridge, MA 02140

Text copyright © 1998 by Stella Blackstone Illustrations copyright © 1998 by Debbie Harter
Translation by Servane Champion

The moral rights of Stella Blackstone and Debbie Harter have been asserted.

First published in Great Britain by Barefoot Books Ltd in 1998 and 2001 and in the United States of America
by Barefoot Books Inc in 1998. This edition published in 2009

This book has been printed in China by Printplus Ltd on 100% acid-free paper

ISBN 978-1-84686-386-8

1 3 5 7 9 8 6 4 2

British Cataloguing-in-Publication Data:
a catalogue record for this book is available from the British Library

Library of Congress Cataloging-in-Publication Data available under LCCN 299003086